Stolen By Alphas Mate
Wolf Shifter Romance

Amelia Wilson

Table of Contents

Prologue
Chapter 1
Chapter 2
Chapter 3
Chapter 4
Chapter 5
Chapter 6
Chapter 7
Chapter 8
Chapter 9
Epilogue

Copyright © 2020 by Amelia Wilson
All rights reserved.

In no way is it legal to reproduce, duplicate, or transmit any part of this document in either electronic means or in printed format. Recording of this publication is strictly prohibited, and any storage of this document is not allowed unless with written permission from the publisher. All rights reserved.

This book is a work of fiction. Names, characters, places and incidents are either the product of the author's imagination or are used fictitiously, and any resemblance to actual persons, living or dead, events or locales is entirely coincidental.

Prologue

Walking home drunk was never a good idea. Nor was it relaxing. Every rustle of clothing, whispering breeze, and any noise between those sounded so much louder and more menacing with alcohol coursing through a person's system. Everyone talked about the safety aspect of it, but it was the rest that came first. The pounding heart and paranoia. The goosebumps that prickled so sharply as to almost feel painful...

It was a lesson that apparently Mabry was going to have to learn the hard way.

What made it even worse was that she was walking home alone.

Which would have looked more frightening just for that alone, but there were no other bodies also making a similar trek. There were no street lamps to light her way or doorways that she could duck into at the last minute if she really started to feel uncomfortable...

No, that would have made it too simple. It also just so happened that the path back to her dorm cut straight through the woods without so much as stopping for baked pastry goodness at the home of a sweet old Grandmother to feed her and tell her stories about the old days. Instead there was only the sound of crackling branches and rustling leaves. The only light she had to go by was what the stars and moon above provided outside of that very dim glow coming from the phone pressed so tightly to her cheek. It was the makings of every dumb college girl in a horror movie, Mabry knew, because that was exactly what she was saying loudly into her cell phone.

"Keep announcing yourself to everybody on the trail Mabry, that's totally smart," the sarcastic voice on the other end of the phone snorted, exasperation clear in her tone. Becky was having none of Mabry's shit, but that didn't stop her from agreeing to be her sober buddy on the way home, even if it was only over the phone. Despite only knowing one another for a handful of months this year at school, it was like the pair of them had known one another their whole lives. It had been like an act of fate for the two of them to end up assigned to one another.

She really couldn't have asked for a better roommate. Becky was nearly her polar opposite in every way. Where Mabry loved color and light, Becky wore nothing but black and lined her already perfect features into a nearly intimidating sculpture on the daily. She had quickly proven herself to have a sharp tongue and an even sharper mind. Which was very likely why she had remained in the dorms to study for their Sociology exam the next day.

Whereas Mabry was nearly skipping her intoxicated self down the dark, wooded path on her way back to their shared room to gorge on the cookies that she had stuffed under her pillow at two o'clock in the morning.

"At least I take it that things went well then?" Becky prompted, her eye roll so visceral that Mabry could hear it even through the phone.

"Oh Becky, you have no idea how much fun my night has been. When I say perfect, I mean *perfect,*" Mabry gushed excitedly, giggling at the way her voice crashed in waves against the silence of the trees around her.

"It was just a party," Becky muttered in disbelief, but then she and Mabry saw things so very differently.

It might have just been a party had the guest list been different, or if it had gone differently even. Mabry was just sure, just like she had been with Becky though, that tonight had been an intervention of fate. She had been *meant* to go to that party and *meant* to have spilled her drink. The entire course of her life had been altered, she could feel it, and it couldn't just be the alcohol talking.

"Yes, but he was there and there was this *connection*," Mabry explained, her words dropping lower to impart the importance of the word.

"You think that you have a connection with everybody that you find pretty," Becky laughed over the phone, her tone far more lenient than her actual words.

"What's the harm in that?" Mabry demanded, eyes narrowing at what she was conceiving, in the moment, as some sort of rebuff of her emotions.

"The harm is that you're nearly shouting when you should be hustling your pretty ass home to me. We have a movie date," Becky placated, the telltale sound of the microwave beeping in the background signaling that she was already readying the popcorn in preparation.

"I know, I'm -" Mabry's voice cut off with an abrupt, sharp inhale midword. The chipper tones of her laughter fading from her voice as she fell rapidly silent. It was a feat that was normally impossible for Mabry, especially after drinking like she had. She waited a moment, frantic eyes scanning the trees around her before her lowered voice sounded once more. "I think he followed me." Mabry whispered, the barest hint of a giggle working its way beneath her whispered words.

She could hear it as she spoke, those noises that had made her pause so quickly. Leaves rustling and branches snapping, but not in the same ways that had been naturally occurring before. It was more calculated, more deliberate, and much, *much* closer.

"What?" Becky demanded, enough suspicion entering her tone to more than make up for the lack of it in Mabry's own voice.

"I can hear something out in the trees," Mabry whispered again, blinking widely at the too dark landscape. *She could barely make out the individual branches, much less what might lie between them.* It didn't occur to her that the sounds might mean danger. Mabry's brain was still wrapped in a warm haze that was coloring the otherwise foreboding setting that she had put herself in.

Footsteps in the forest like this didn't usually mean something good. In that moment, however, she couldn't see the noise of something slowly tracking her movements from the shadows of the treeline as scary. Only as vaguely playful.

"Mabry...what's happening?" Becky's voice rose.

"Shhh," Maybry whispered back, a little too loudly. "I think he's trying to spook me." It didn't matter that clearly the thing in the forest with her couldn't hear the other end of the phone. Logic had left the building four vodka spritzers before. "COME ON OUT! YOU WILL HAVE TO TRY HARDER THAN THAT MASON!" She called out suddenly, laughter filling the words as she spun about, grinning into the empty air as if the challenge were about to be met by the tall, roguish junior she had spent the majority of her night with.

    Mabry stumbled, one foot over the other before catching herself, her palm scraping against the rough bark of the tree she used to steady herself. Her phone fell out of her hand as she brought the index finger of the same hand over her lips to 'hush' herself, giggling. "Oh shoot." She realized that she had dropped her phone just a moment too late.

    The rustling from the trees seemed closer now. Branches cracking under the footfall of something heavy. A large shadow moving in the space around her as Mabry attempted to bend to grab her phone from the ground without falling over herself.

    She was so preoccupied that she didn't even see the sudden burst of movement until it was too late. A massive fur covered body erupted in a flurry of teeth and claws, launching toward her slender frame with an impossible speed and knocking her back off of her feet before she could even register that it had happened outside of the breath being knocked out of her so effectively. Her back hit the compact earth, sharp inhale her response to the anguish that radiated from between her shoulder blades at the crash landing- fingers catching ineffectively against handfuls of short, soft fur.

  The connection of teeth into her flesh was instantly sobering, searing pain as her skin split beneath the bite, gaze swimming. Mabry's back arched against the attack, her head throwing back and mouth slanting open in a terrified, wounded wail… but her scream was only heard by the birds and one terrified, helpless friend on the other end of a phone so suddenly crushed under the weight of Mabry's attacker. That and the creature that had pinned and bitten her so effectively...

  The creature shifted as that scream petered out, Mabry's form drooping unconsciously within its grasp as it shifted, moving off of her only to begin dragging her body from where it's teeth still gripped her. The shattered glass shards spread with the movement of the two bodies, a crimson trail painted under and around it as the two of them disappeared entirely from sight. Come morning that trail would be all of Mabry that could be found.

Chapter 1

"People will be looking for me!" The blonde girl screamed from within the enclosure. She didn't know where she was being kept, or even in what. It was a room that was to be sure, but there were no identifying features within it. Packed earth made up the flooring and the walls were as bare as they were wooden. It was the room that she had woken up in, disoriented and injured, her head pounding for a multitude of reasons that she couldn't even begin to unpack. There had been no explanation, no bandaging, nothing other than the room and her body.

Mabry had been shouting insults for what felt like hours. She had started with questions, the sound of someone moving from the other side of the door the only response it seemed they deemed necessary to give her. That questioning had turned to begging- and the beginning very quickly to her verbal outrage. She had used every profanity that she could think of and then some. Each ignored slight only made it worse though, screaming out new, invented insults and threatening each and everything that she could call to mind. Dismemberment, bodily harm, promising them money. The truth of the matter was, though, she didn't know who was holding her captive. So she didn't know which route would really be the most effective. She had just been clinging to the hope that at least since somebody knew that she was missing, somebody should be looking for her.

Everything was dark around her. Shades of black and gray that her gaze couldn't penetrate no matter how hard she tried. She only knew that she was laying next to a door because what little light came from beneath the crack in it was the only source of light in the room. Wherever she was being held didn't have so much as a blanket on the floor for her to take comfort in, no furniture. Compact earth, wooden walls, and her body. She was so cold that her bones felt brittle, skin that desperate sort of heated it got when trying to regulate against arctic temperatures.

It must have been two days, maybe three? She couldn't keep track of time without any passing markers. Perhaps it had been even longer, there really was no telling anymore.

All she knew was that she was cold, tired, and hungry. The room that she was being held in didn't let too much sound in, not outside of that faint movement she had heard before, but she could see the bodies crossing in front of the door every now and again. Quick, flashing shadows that blocked her already limited source even more. They never stopped though, never stayed for longer than it took for them to shove food into the slot under the door the very few times that they did.

I have been kidnapped. It was the one and only thing that she could be certain of.

The memories of how it had happened were fuzzy, she needed to put all of the pieces together, but her head hurt. Varying red hues of scrapes marked her arms and hands from where she must have fallen. There was even a large knot on her forehead above her eye and tender spots dotting the back of her head… though the worst was her shoulder.

She didn't know how deep the cuts were there near her clavicle. They formed a half circle into her skin. If she didn't think that it was absolutely crazy she would have sworn that it felt like teeth marks. She was in bad shape.

No time for crying Mabry, pull it together.

At least the punctures on her abdomen seemed to have stopped bleeding.

What do they want from me?

It could have been anything. Left alone like this for so long her imagination had started to run wild. She was a nobody. She was a scholarship kid whose family hadn't come from money. Her parents didn't have fancy or important jobs. She wasn't even the best student. Whatever they had taken her for, it couldn't be with the hopes of earning a ransom. It didn't matter what she was yelling, she didn't even know if they were listening to her in the first place.

Frustration came anew as she attempted to kick defiantly at the door through the tears that threatened to blot out the single line of light from her vision.

"What do you want from me?!" she sobbed in spite of herself, her body curling in on itself for heat as her body succumbed to exhaustion.

Mabry awoke violently to the sound of the door to her room being ripped open, the door crashing against the wooden walls that had served as her cell the last few days. She couldn't see right away, green eyes rejecting the sudden influx of light that came with the intrusion and her arm lifting to shield them on instinct. She was too frightened to have the sense to scream, or even the will to do so as two large bodies crowded into the room with her. Without any explanation or pause their meaty palms wrapped about her forearms, lifting her from the ground she had been laying on roughly.

The pain in her abdomen burned to life with the sudden movement, torn muscles trying to tense themselves and finding nothing but a clawing sensation in their place. She shook from the force of it, groaning in pain as they wasted no time in hauling her from the space she had become so familiar with and down a long, concrete hallway. Recessed light fixtures dotted the ceiling above them, but there were no other doors that she could see on either side of them even as she frantically turned her head in an effort to do so. There were no signs on the walls or anything else that might help to tell her where she was. The hallway was just as barren and empty as the room she had been being held in had been, save for the light that was allowed into it. Actually, it looked like every secret underground bunker from every movie that she had ever seen.

She squirmed as best she could from within their tight grasps, trying not to ignite those injuries any more than their treatment was already causing. She wanted to ask questions. She wanted to demand to know who they were and where they were taking her. She wanted to plead with them to let her go and explain that if only they would let her go, that she would never say anything to anyone ever.

She needed to tell them that she needed a doctor.

But fear held her tongue locked to the roof of her mouth. Fear and the memory of her trying all of those things from behind that door and being so easily ignored.

"Put her over here," a gruff voice commanded. The man speaking was tall, his skin littered with scars and tattoos too numerous to see where the ink started and torn skin stopped. Like a rough biker-king, but it was beautiful all on its own. He was handsome and she hated that her vanity made her feel a little less afraid from that fact alone. Something about his eyes was almost kind, or perhaps it was remorse hiding behind those brown depths in the way that he regarded her as she was drug into the space.

The two men on either side of her guided Mabry into a space close to that bonfire, fingers releasing her so suddenly and without warning that her entire body just collapsed to the ground. Her palms hit hard, pushing into the earth despite how bruised that skin felt as she struggled to push herself upright.

"I'm sorry for the manner that we've had to keep you until now," the speaker intoned, voice lowering somewhat as he stepped only near enough to her to be easily heard. A social sort of distance in a situation that didn't regard any of the other usual rules. "In time you will see that we had no choice," he promised, an apologetic tilt to his lips. "You were never supposed to be here."

Mabry didn't know how to take his words, or even the man in front of her. Her arms wrapped about herself as she finally pushed herself upright, straightening her spine and pushing back in an attempt to keep as much heat from the bonfire in her pores as was humanly possible as she watched the man speak. Nobody else was moving, no other noise other than the speaker's voice and that gentle crackle of the fire behind it. He was the only one speaking and for the life of her she couldn't force words out of her mouth in order to answer him.

"We had to ensure that nobody was going to come looking for you," he explained, his chin dipping forward. Like he knew the reaction that his words were going to have.

She wished that she could have reacted differently, but the words were like pins being pushed into a balloon. The last vestiges of hope bled rapidly out of her body, shoulders sagging at how final his tone was. He just seemed so very sure, phrasing it in the way that he had, and if nobody really was coming after her… then how was she ever going to get out of this?

He cleared his throat some, moving on as if she hadn't just partially crumpled where she sat. "While this wasn't planned, you do provide a really unique opportunity for our pack here, and while it's going to be confusing for you at first… in time you will come to understand. Our pack has been struggling for some time, you see. Our numbers aren't what they used to be and we wolves are a dying breed." There was a rustling with his words, like they were painful to those listening.

But Mabry didn't understand. *Wolves? What did that mean? They weren't wolves. They were human.*

"Sascha bit you because she smelled the chance that you carried for our pack," the man continued to explain to her, his own nostrils flaring somewhat as if he were smelling that very same thing. "Pups come so few and far between… and while this was no doubt not the life that you had imagined for yourself, you will serve a purpose so much larger than any that you could begin to imagine." His tone became almost reverent, even if still half-laced with apology. There was a fervor behind his eyes and words both, his eyes imploring her to understand. But what was she supposed to be understanding? *His words didn't even make any sense!*

"You can provide us with those pups to regrow our numbers… and in doing so you will be allowed to earn a place here in your new pack." He moved to kneel in front of her as he spoke, his curled finger coming to lift her chin as he delivered his final words. "After you've transitioned, of course."

What? The hell was that supposed to mean!?

Mabry still found herself unable to speak, her chest heaving as her breath came in shorter and shorter gasps. She was desperately trying to understand what he meant, or what the words he was using could stand for. *Wolves? Pups? Surely he couldn't be referring to what he seemed to be*. As obvious as it seemed her mind couldn't possibly comprehend another human actually believing in what it was he seemed to be stating was fact.

Her mind spun, jaw clenching as she wrenched her face out of his grasp violently, head almost shaking. She wanted it to be a lie. She wanted to think that he was lying to her, but why would he? He had the upper hand here, he and those people he was with, she was just one unarmed, college aged girl. *So why would he?* It was too crazy. This entire situation was insane. She was dreaming. She absolutely had to be dreaming. Some frantic, alcohol induced nightmare from her walk home or something.

Black dots began pin pricking her vision, circling and enlarging in such random order that it only served to disorient her even further. He couldn't- the thought shifted, trailing off even mentally at the blackness stole her again, her body collapsing to the side in a heap upon the ground with her eyes rolling all the way back into her skull.

Chapter 2

The moon hung heavy over the tops of the trees, opalescent in hue against the cloudy black sky around it- stars all but blotted out by that coverage. It was the kind of night that swallowed you whole, pulling you into its embrace until nothing but the whites of one's eyes could be seen. The forest as a whole held its breath, creatures large and small turned in whether they be nocturnal or otherwise.

In the middle of the expanse there was too much noise, howling and hollering, music reverberating off of the bark of the trees around it.. The fires lit in the glade that night were bright enough to almost completely obscure that darkness over the treetops, their heat combined with all of those over-heated bodies in the clearing making it a near sweltering blanket; even though it was in the midst of late autumn.

Wolves fit between all of those fires, between trees and tents- their half-covered bodies shimmering with beads of sweat as they danced and sung raucously, feasting on what had been prepared that night. It was a celebration- and a large one. But then, the pack hosting it was large.

Horas hadn't been in these parts since their alpha had been newly blooded, passing through even as he was now. Only, the changes that the pack had undergone were abundant and obvious. It had always been one of the wilder packs, large and numerous, with very little attention paid to common decorum and correctness…

Now it was even more rabid, more ferally apparent in even just the way the wolves conducted themselves. Before there had been an even mixture of genders and many pups running between the legs of those older than them… and now there didn't seem to be any pups younger than their teen years, and for every one woman there seemed to be another six males surrounding her. The scars shared between them, woman or man, would have put even long hardened veterans to shame.

It wasn't what he had been expecting, coming here.

Neither was the celebration. It was no full moon, no holiday either. It was a capture celebration, the Alpha had informed him, her teeth glinting in the late evening sun as she had grinned at him. Capture. Even the one word felt foreign to his mind. It wasn't unheard of, at least not historically, for packs to start taking young, fertile women when it was that their own packs began to dwindle…

But that had been seventy years or more past since it had been a common practice.

The bare soles of his feet were light, whisper silent as he walked over the forest floor- grass turning to dirt- and dirt to twig as he circled further and further away from that celebration. Towards the huts. *And the pit.* A crude agglomeration of stick and stone woven together in such a way to resemble spikes, with only the one entry or exit chained so tightly and held together with a large, iron lock. I*t was a prison cell, not a pit.*

It was a *cage.*

He couldn't have named what drew him in that direction other than a sick sense of curiosity, following that well tread path until he was near even with the walls of the cage, catching sight of that slight body huddled within to one corner and allowing the arm holding his mug of ale to drop slightly. He had been expecting the sight to be jarring.

What he hadn't expected was that smell.

So staggeringly robust that his feet nearly missed a step as he came to a complete halt. It was like hot pressed honey-cakes and old coffee, the faintest hint of vanilla mixed beneath it with a breath of cinnamon. He felt like it was going to cripple him. He felt like the scent alone would bring him to his knees and force a full body spasm. *She smelled like home.*

Which was absolutely impossible and more than a little concerning. A very large part of him wanted to turn tail and run in the opposite direction, visiting pack be damned, connection be damned. He had been alone for forty odd years, travelling between packs since he had come of age to do so, going where and when he pleased… *He didn't need a mate.* He had never even sought one, but the scent didn't lie.

His gravity shifted, nostrils flaring as the girl turned, her blue-green eyes lighting against his and the air rushing out of his chest in an undignified huff. He said nothing. Still and silent as she looked around, body straightening from the way she had been bent and hesitantly approaching where he stood, each movement more careful than the last. Like a frightened rabbit having seen a fox, but too stupid to walk away.

A low growl built in his chest, but he restrained it, swallowing back the urge and cocking his head. "What's your name, girl?" he asked instead, the barest hint of that growl present beneath his words.

Those eyes he was so locked into flashed- unnamed hidden emotion that moved so quickly through her as to be masked by the scent of fear and trepidation that hung so thickly around her like a cloud he couldn't sniff it out. "Mabry," she muttered, her head tilting slightly, narrowed eyes looking him over.

Mabry. Like the syrup. Mable syrup. He almost snorted, taking a step closer to the cage and thrusting his drink through it. "Mabry," he muttered. "Here. Not right that you should be left out when the celebration is for you," he nodded, indicating his drink even if his words were a dark sort of sarcastic.

Her eyes moved from him to the area around them, darting back and forth before shuffling forward that slightest bit more, taking the cup and holding it in her hands though she made no move to drink from it. She could keep smelling like that though. Fear and confusion. It was near heady, the way it mixed with that attraction for her scent so strongly that dual instincts were enraptured at once. To chase and protect. Prey and mate.

"Celebration?" Her grief was clearly stamped over her features as she spoke with a too dry throat. "They are celebrating my kidnapping?" Her nose crinkled when she spoke, tears threatening her eyes at the rims. "Or my torture?" She sounded like she couldn't believe that anybody could be so horrible.

"Torture?" he echoed her, eyebrows knitting together. He saw no evidence of that on her body, or smelt it either, but maybe that was due to the fact that she was so close to her first Turn. "They are celebrating your addition to the pack," he informed her slowly, not that she had made it yet, but that was what it was. "How you came to be pack and the circumstances surrounding it do not matter to them." His shoulders rolled in a loose shrug, eyes breaking from hers for the tension that it caused his chest, a tight line between the two of their bodies that he was trying to keep from acknowledging. "You are fertile and young, two things their bitches can no longer claim."

The nose made in the back of her throat signaled to how unbelieveable she found her situation. Despair was scenting off of her in waves. She didn't look like she believed a word coming out of his mouth.

"What's your name?" she asked after a half moment, sloshing the contents of that cup and lifting her eyes to him almost hesitantly. *He would eat her.* Open those bars and let her loose into the night so that he could hunt her down.

He stifled that as well, clearing his throat and dropping down to his haunches, knees bent and his hands hanging loosely between them as he rested his forearms on his thighs. "Horas." Short and simple. He gave her no more than she had given him.

"Well Horas-" she started, only to be cut off the minute that his chin jerked to the side, nostrils flaring again as he stood just as quickly from that relaxed stance as he had dropped into it. His shoulders tensed, nose twitching as he paced away from that cage. One step and then three, nostrils flaring as he scented the wind.

"Wait! Please, get me out of here."

"Later, little she-wolf. When their fires die low- and their pack goes to sleep. I'll come back then." His words were quicker then, hinted accent shining through the way that he spoke, his pupils dilating and growing in rapid order just as the sounds of that snarling and yelping began to reach them. "Drink, it'll make the noises easier," he offered, voice dropping only slightly in kindness before his whole body shifted, muscles dancing beneath taut skin as his hands moved to the band of his jeans- pushing them down his hips only moments before he sprang forward.

Skin melded to fur, hand to claw, and nose to muzzle, yellow eyes flashing in the dark of the night as he sprinted from where he had been standing before, body disappearing into the trees once more as one long, low scream rent the air.

Chapter 3

There were no words for what she had just seen. Mabry hadn't even been sure that the scream wasn't her own for a long moment after he had left. It had left. Whatever it was. The words from the past few days fusing with what she had witnessed melded together in her mind until the one word kept rebounding throughout her thoughts like a reverberating echo.

Werewolf.

She was in a movie. Perhaps a very, very bad dream. The explosion of skin into fur as that body who had tried talking to her, Horas, had left her just as suddenly as he had come. It made everything seem so much more real. Wolf and pups. Suddenly all of those things that had been told to her before made more sense, the promise of how important she was going to become and how much bigger a purpose she would serve. She still didn't understand, but what was beginning to make sense was far more frightening than she had even begun to imagine before. She didn't even have the mental capacity to ruminate on the promise to return that he had made her right before leaving as he had.

It had been such a simple gesture to him it seemed like. One minute he had been flesh and bone- like her, and the next he had been a giant wolf bounding off into the darkness of the night after those sounds of screaming and fighting that had sounded so demonic to her ears. Like his changing skin like that was as easy and normal as breathing... Yet to her, it made a nightmare of her entire future. Horas was the only one to have even waited for her to speak this entire time, the only one to speak to her in any way that had even allowed for a response. That didn't make him any better than the rest of them, but it did give her something to cling to.

Was she going to become like that though? Was she going to turn into one of these creatures that seemed to have zero regard for human life? She hadn't been attended to by a nurse or a medic or a medicine person, nothing at all. They hadn't fed her or given her clothing that wasn't damaged to cover herself with. It was as if they had no regard whatsoever for her injuries or her capture in the first place. Like it was just… normalized.

Her body shook, fingers curling into her palms as her mind reeled. This 'shift' that they kept talking about, they meant her turning into a wolf. Like them. Like she had just seen of Horas. She didn't feel like she could accept that as fact, like it could really be happening to her at all. She was cold, hurt, and hungry. The same three emotions echoing from her captivity of before to the one they were now keeping her in outdoors. It didn't matter that the setting had shifted, or that at least out here she could see. She was still being held prisoner.

She sank back into the cold earth, green eyes watching the spectacle of this 'celebration'.

The bodies around those fires that she could see danced well into the night, shadows weaving in and out of her sight as the sounds of their merriment filled the forest. Ever so occasionally one of those bodies would follow the path to find her there in the darkness, eyes glowing varied shades of yellow from where they stood. Their responses seemed just as varied as their eye color- though they tended to mostly fit between two categories: gushing gratitude and jeering laughter.

The worst of them were the bodies that came *together* though. Stripping down outside of the cage and forcing their naked bodies as if they wanted her to watch and listen. She was only forced to do the former, turning her gaze away with red cheeks and an uncomfortable dropping in her belly each time it was that it happened. It was the only thing that made her thankful for her lack of food from that celebration, afraid that she would have lost it after the second such couple.

They just kept claiming that she was good luck, rubbing those bars and asking her for their blessing. Assuring one another and her that being so near her fruitful womb would bless them into children of their own, without having need of using her later. Perhaps they were barren for a reason though. Monsters like this should never have been allowed to have bred in the first place. They certainly shouldn't have allowed this treatment of her. Barren or not.

She wanted to go home.

You really are just a stupid, careless girl, aren't you?

The longer the dark grew the harder it was getting to stand. Each passing minute made her limbs feel more and more like lead and she was beginning to think that it had very little at all to do with the hunger. The teeth and claw marks on her body didn't even hurt anymore. Mabry had given up trying to figure out if she was just numbing from the cold or if it was somehow getting better, green eyes watching those fires die one by one… Breathing was getting easier at least.

Even if she was beginning to also give up on Horas coming back…

He had probably found something somewhere out in that celebration that better caught his attention than talking to the captive. Somewhere more suited to his needs than listening to her complain. Maybe he had been lying about all of it in the first place and had just wanted a closer look at her- to suss her out for future breeding stock. *He probably just wanted first dibs.* Her thoughts grew more and more cynical the more that her body ached. Like something was pushing and tearing at her skin from the inside out…

The moon shifted in the sky slowly, that last fire dying out and with it very nearly that last strand of hope that she had been holding onto so firmly. She didn't even know why she wanted Horas to come back so badly… she just knew that she did. The bags under her eyes grew deeper and darker and… she swore that she could hear soft footsteps approaching her, approaching the cage- and she nearly backed away from that door in response. Only the face that appeared was the one that she had been so desperately waiting on. And even from the distance he was coming she almost swore that she could *smell* him. The lack of sleep had to be playing with her mind...

"You look like hell," he greeted without ceremony, his tone gruff and his words more blunt than she had been expecting. She didn't know what he wanted, or why he was looking at her in the way that he was, his dark eyes hooded and intense as he stopped just in front of that door to her enclosure. Four words and they made her bristle and glare with a righteous sort of indignation as she stared him back down.

Her eyes narrowed, chin lifting as she only just stopped herself from sneering at him. She couldn't even summon the words to explain how crazy that sounded given her circumstances. Of course she looked like hell. "Then let me go," she countered, forcing more bravado into her voice than she actually felt.

Horas snorted, his fluorescent yellow eyes flashing with some unnamed emotion as he looked her over again, nostrils flaring. She wasn't sure if that was supposed to have been amused or upset, his facial features held so tightly that she couldn't hope to even try reading them. "That's not my decision," he said slowly, his tone as guarded as his words seemed to be. One shoulder lifted, a half-shrug encompassing the one side of his body before he glanced behind him to where all of those voices had finally died down in the past few hours. "You haven't slept?"

He tacked the question onto the end of his statement as if he had only just noticed it and again she was taken aback. What kind of question was that? What kind of answer was that for a response to what she had said even?! "What do you mean it's not your decision," she demanded hotly, dirt encrusted fingers wrapping around those bars of her cage as she hauled herself closer. "You can't just keep people in cages!" Her words were harried, desperation filling her every word and clawing up the back of her throat painfully. Of course she hadn't slept, she was terrified.

Horas snorted, though that time it almost sounded like a growl to her, eyes shooting up to the way that his flashed again. She didn't have to question that emotion, at least not on the surface, he almost looked angry, and she had to fight the temptation to scurry back away from it. "I'm not keeping you anywhere, girl," he informed her, words stressed. "Didn't take you. Not my pack, not my rules. And technically, right now, you're just a human. Your rights aren't the same."

Mabry's eyes grew wide, dry lips parting in a surprised sort of 'o'. "My rights?" She echoed, as if she couldn't comprehend what he was talking about, because she couldn't. Not really. She didn't understand how he could use those words with her body in the shape it was in, with how she had been dragged her against her will and held so inhumanely. "My right is to not be kidnapped! My right is to not be *mauled* when walking home at night. My rights!" she cut off, scoff dying in her throat at the way that his head tilted, regarding her in a way that made the hair on the back of her neck stand up.

"You're human," he said simply, as if that were an explanation for everything. "You don't understand... You have no rights. Them taking you like this is considered an honor. To you. Allowing you the chance to join their pack and bear their pups- an honor. Until your first shift you are nothing more than a human, no matter how close to that shift you are." Again his nostrils flared and she was left wondering if he were *smelling* her? Was that something that he could smell? How close to her 'shift' she was?

He said it all so bluntly, as if it were just fact, and she didn't know how she knew that he wasn't saying it to be hurtful, but she did. It was that fact that made her sag even more. "I don't want this," she admitted in a suddenly small voice, her eyes brimming with unshed tears. "I don't want... anything that they said was going to happen to me," she choked out, voice dying out with an undignified sort of squeak. It was too real, the emotion too present, and suddenly even making eye contact hurt, her eyes dropping to the ground beneath her feet as she fought openly crying. She had done enough of that.

"You don't have a choice with that part," Horas said slowly, his voice very nearly sympathetic. "You were bitten. It doesn't matter what you do now, short of ending your own life, you will still shift. In here- in this cage- or out there…" he trailed off, eyes blazing into her own when she did dare to lift her chin in question at his words.

Her thoughts tumbled, a tangled mass of too much information and not enough time to process it, lips opening and her eyes darting behind him. "You you aren't one of them…" she trailed off, unsure how she was so sure that she could trust his words… "How can you just stand by?" The burning question filtered from her so quickly that she almost blurred her words together, a disappointed note of betrayal that she had no right or reason to feel filling in beneath her words.

"There are laws," he said gently, his voice dropping in a way that she hadn't yet heard it do. "What they are doing, here, with you… it doesn't go against them. It is a Right. An old, old right. Even if it is outdated," Horas trailed off momentarily again, his gaze intent on her face, on the expressions that passed over it as he spoke. "I haven't seen it enacted outside of this pack in more than seventy years, but that doesn't change our laws. It doesn't make it disappear just because it becomes uncommon."

Seventy years?! He hardly looked older than her, how could he state that so surely? How could he say that he hadn't seen it since then? She took a half step back, her hands falling from the bars and her gaze sharpening with a disbelief that was quickly melding into suspicion. "So you do this then? This is what you get off on? Watching girls kept in cages and-" she stopped, the words drying in her throat for what she knew that she would have said next. Mabry still, even in the face of all of it, was unable to admit out loud just what it was that they wanted her for…

"Watch what you're inferring," Horas growled, taking that half-step forward to make up for the distance she had tried to put between them. "I didn't put you in that cage, I didn't take you, girl. I am a visitor here. I don't have to be talking to you or explaining things…" he warned her, that anger clear, but not in the way that she had been expecting. It seemed more offended than anything else and that didn't make sense to her either.

Mabry's own features shifted, her eyebrows pinching as she tried to understand what he was saying. "Why are you then?" she finally asked, confusion lining the words nearly as fully as that emotional distress was. She watched the way that he eyed her after her question, lips pulling as if he were unsure which words to use, and all it did was serve to make her even more curious.

"Just because it isn't against our laws doesn't mean that there aren't still many out there who don't disagree with the practice. There is a reason why it is no longer so widely exercised." He spoke so carefully and surely that it forced her to pay even more attention to his words. *No longer widely exercised*, he said it as if that was important and all that it did was make her question it even further. *Did that mean that most wolves didn't do this?*

Mabry moved over to the door of the cage where Horas was standing, trying to get a better look at his face. She had no idea if he was telling the truth now or if, in fact, he had been down there doing just as much as the others had been. If he was conning her somehow now… She didn't even know what she would do. He was the first person to speak to her as if she were a person as well, the first person to treat her with any sort of equality and that made her even more dubious. Her arms crossed over her midsection, defending herself both from that cold and that pervasive uneasiness that trembled through her every muscle.

Her hand moved to the bar of that cage, wrapping around it as she looked up at him. "Then just let me go," she pleaded, choosing to believe him. Choosing to believe the fact that he hadn't put her here or wanted her here, that he disagreed with that practice as much as it sounded like he did. She didn't want to be passed around and used to breed their 'pups'. She didn't want to stay with them at all. "Please," she begged, tremor building beneath the one word. "You can just open the door…" And she would do the rest. She would run, as fast and as hard as she could in the opposite direction. She just needed a chance.

His chin dropped though, shaking his head even as she spoke. "I open this door and you go off running on your own…" he trailed off, a violent edge hardening his expression as he tore his gaze from hers, looking back in the direction that those wolves lay. "They will chase you down and drag you back," he finished, voice laden with promise as he looked seriously back at her, imparting those words with a sense of overwhelming finality. "You think what you face now is bad?" he barked a laugh, merciless and cold. "Girl, you have no idea how bad it can get. Have you not seen the scars that mark their skin? Don't be fooled by their fur, they are not puppies you can play with. They are wolves. And battle hardened wolves at that…"

She swayed on her feet, hand falling from the bars as her feet gave way from beneath her. There was no doubting the truth to his words at that. Even just hearing him say it like he had she could see the images of their scar riddled skin in her memory, bright and brilliant hues against their differing skin tones… She had thought that it was just wolves in general, based off of what she had seen. But looking at Horas now she realized that while, yes, scarring was there, it was nothing compared to those others that had jeered from outside of the cage that weren't him.

This was her fate. She was helpless and they would do whatever the chose to with her.

Mabry's face crumpled, her soft features giving way to tears even as she sunk down into the earth beneath her. *That was it then*. The fight diminished from even a slight hope, the conversation and reality crushing down on her like a large boulder that she couldn't hope to move. Not even that bone deep exhaustion stopped those silent, grief ridden sobs from racking her body.

Chapter 4

Damnit. Horas had battled all night with that desire to return to the girl in this cage. Mabry. Mabry, his mate, which was still a fact that set unsteadily in his gullet as if just waiting to be expelled. Even as far away from her as he had gone to attend that fight, when he had left her he had known. He had smelled her still, on his fur, in the air- that sweet, heady scent that clung to her and her alone. *Mate.* There was no denying such indisputable fact. It was genetically wired into him, a gift from the gods, and yet so terribly unexpected...

And in such circumstances as these... dangerous.

He had intended to just speak to her, but watching her crumble like that tore away at his stomach lining like caustic acid, whole body rejecting the fact that he had been the one to distress her like that. He shifted, eyes closing and his fingers twitching at his side as he inhaled. Steady breaths to try and put himself back on an even emotional keel. He swore he could feel her, that distress tearing through her, echoing within his own chest...

Horas crossed what little space was left between he and that cage door, fingers extended until they could wrap about the lock that hung off of it, and his wrist jerking it near immediately. It wasn't designed to hold wolves, not this chain, the rusted lock breaking apart within his fingers and falling to the ground with a resounding thunk that lifted Mabry's head from the dejected way it had fallen. Her wide green eyes took in his movements, lips parting and a rough breath exhaling past them.

"Get up," Horas commanded, gravel abrading his tone for that worry that filled him. *This was breaking the law.* This was not how this was supposed to be handled, and this pack was large enough that should he be caught… their justice would be swift and final. They didn't need Horas the way that they needed Mabry. "And be quick about it," he added, ignoring the way that her body trembled as she tried to unsuccessfully rise from where she had fallen. He couldn't afford to comfort or placate her now, not with what all factors were set against them.

They needed to move quickly and silently if they were going to move at all.
Her legs shook, her hands finally pushing down hard enough to allow her to rise into a standing position, half-leaning on those bars as she set her equilibrium back to

rights. Again, her mouth opened, green eyes looking over him with a cross of emotions that he couldn't pause to try and decipher now. And yet again, no sound actually left her.

"Can you run?" he asked, brushing past her awkward pause as his gaze roved over the perimeter with a kind of wary severity. "We won't make it far with you walking like that," he admitted, gaze swinging frankly back to hers. They wouldn't make it very far with her walking at all. She was going to need to run, and with more balance than she currently was just standing with as well.

He could hear her heart racing, blood pounding through her veins even from this distance with how high her anxiety had spiked. Fear smelt good on her, wicking off of her and easing out of her pores in thick plumes, deepening that vanilla that clung to the edges of her scent. It was entirely the wrong time for him to be taking notice of that smell and for his body to be responding to it in the way that it was. *He would devour her whole.* His tongue ran along the sharpened point of one canine, smoothing over that jagged edge before watching her nod determinedly in a way that didn't at all match her scent.

"Then run," he prompted, fingertips pushing hard into the small of her back in an attempt to shove her into motion. "Don't stop. Don't look back. Don't slow down," he instructed, voice level and severe to match the solemnity of the situation. "You run," he spun her body just enough to keep her from that more densely populated piece of forest floor that all of those sleeping bodies were piled atop one another in the aftermath of the celebration. "That way. Don't stop unless your legs give out." He was already moving away from the cage himself, muscles rounding and bunching beneath his skin in preparation.

  She moved easily enough, readying herself as if she too were about to run, but at the last second she paused, green eyes lifting to his as if she couldn't help herself. "Why did you change your mind?" she asked low-voiced, lips thinning out. He couldn't help but notice that faint, incandescent yellowing ring that had begun to build up within her iris… She was so close, it had to only be strength of will alone that was keeping her from changing between her two skins at this point.

  "Who said I changed it?" he challenged, eyebrows half lifting as he deliberated telling her himself. Something about the way she was regarding him told him to tread carefully. After the events of the past few days and the things that she had been told by the wolves of this pack he wasn't sure that hearing anything about her being his mate would go over well.

She didn't say anything though, even with the way she eyed him as if she knew that he was leaving something out. Maybe she did. He didn't know how far that bond stretched given that she was still technically human. He didn't know if she could even feel it yet…

But before he could question her on any of it she had spun about on her heel, running awkwardly as quickly as she could in the direction that he had pointed her. He watched her for a moment, heat moving throughout his body at the sight. He hadn't been wrong earlier, the sight of her running the same as the scent of her fear for him.

The instinct to chase her was strong, making his legs lengthen and his abdomen tighten. He wanted to tackle her back down to that ground and remove that scent of those others who had touched her since coming here from her skin. He wanted to claim her as his own. It was a heady imagining, the idea of what her fear and lust would smell like combined.

Even just thinking about it made his nostrils flare, body springing into life behind hers and sprinting off after her. Only he didn't give into those urges, no matter how strong they were. He just ran behind her, for as long as it took before the inevitable happened and her body began to give out, legs giving way under her and his body overtaking hers just in time to scoop her before she connected with the earth beneath her.

Horas didn't say anything, or even acknowledge whatever weak apology she might have been attempting to stutter out. He hadn't been lying about their being pressed for time, nor the real danger that could come if that pack noticed her missing before there was enough distance between them. It would have been easier to shift and run with her like that. Easier and faster, but he didn't think that she would go as willingly were that the case…

So he ran, her body thrown half over his back and the heat of her burning through the thin layer of clothing that he still wore, reminding him of her presence each time that she shifted or was jostled by his steps. It was only when he heard the way that her stomach began gurgling, a weak, empty chain of sounds leaving her, that he reassessed their surroundings and decided that they were far enough to stop for at least a little while.

Not that there was much of a decision to be making, the way that she sounded… Running with her so close to him, with her scent invading his senses and the feel of her body jostling against his, had proven more difficult than he had anticipated. That primal urge to make her his own and claim her, especially given the circumstances in which they had come to meet, had been near unbearable.

    He slowed his steps, waiting until he found a softer, quieter copse of trees that he could come to a complete halt in. He dropped her unceremoniously onto her ass, striding several paces away before he allowed himself to breathe again, a rough sort of exhale that shook through his chest. "You need to eat," he said, breaking the silence. He offered her nothing else but those four words, referencing none of what they had gone through or the trail of the past few days.

    If she kept going too long without food it would only make that eventual shift all the worse for it, and her weak enough that recovering would slow them down even further. As if on cue her stomach rumbled, a loud, foreign noise in the lushly populated copse they had paused in. "Aren't they going to follow us?"

    Her voice was laden with exhaustion, so much so that her earlier fear was nearly muted by it, even in her scent. He turned to her with the question, finally allowing his eyes to rove over her for the first time since he had scooped her up before. "Maybe, maybe not," he answered slowly. He didn't necessarily want to force that fear back into her system, but he didn't want to lie to her either.

"It depends on how long it takes them to notice that you're missing," he continued, making sure she was actually coherent enough to understand his words. "We have a good head start so far… but we can't keep going if you haven't eaten," his yellow gaze took in those dark, purpling bruises beneath her eyes, nostrils flaring at the sight. "Or slept." He watched her sink further into the ground, her shoulders nearly shaking with the effort of staying upright.

"More so with the first," he said with a small frown. She looked half-dead, staring up at him like she was. But she had to eat, that first turn was going to require tremendous amounts of energy, and looking at her now he could see that yellow ring within her iris had grown even further in only the time since they had left.

"It'll go faster if I leave you," he admitted, but even the tenor of his voice betrayed how little he liked that plan. His only placation for it was the spike in fear filtering through her scent at the mention of him leaving her. He didn't want to be separated from her either… but her eating was a necessity, and he couldn't hunt with her with him. It just meant that they were going to have to find a place for her to hide while he was gone to make the both of them feel more secure in it.

"Up in the trees maybe," he offered, gaze turning up to them as if trying to verify that they would hold her weight.

"Is this a good time to mention my fear of heights?" she interjected, voice small and uncertain enough that his hardened features softened somewhat, looking back down to her with a small twitch of his lips even in the circumstances.

"No, it's a terrible time really," he replied dryly, the briefest flash of humor flickering over his features as he turned more fully to her, already trying to think of another option, and failing.

"I was afraid you would say that," she muttered, eyes lifting to the trees surrounding them apprehensively. Concern deepened that bitter note of her scent, Horas' eyes watching as she pulled her lower lip in between her teeth.

"If you're too afraid you won't sleep," he admitted after a moment, his gaze breaking from her worried countenance to look around the clearing once more speculatively. He hadn't been entirely sure that she would have had enough strength to climb any of those trees in the first place, much less hold herself from falling from them should she fall asleep. It was just the safest vantage point that he could think of.

"We need to find a different solution then," he continued, legs lengthening so that he could pace that outline of the space that they had stopped, analyzing each dip and divet large enough to fit her body. He was asking a lot of her, to trust him so quickly, and he knew it. But he also knew that they had little other option, given those that would soon be pursuing them if they hadn't already begun.

He turned back to find Mabry eyeing him as speculatively as he had been their surroundings, a strange expression and even stranger scent encompassing her that he didn't quite recognize. "Okay," she agreed distractedly, swallowing as she glanced away. "Thank you," she tacked on, skin pinkening along the base of her throat and up.

She was blushing.

He bit back a growl, his tongue pressing to the roof of his mouth to stop from commenting on it. "Don't do that," he corrected her instead. He had told her once not to thank him until they were safe, and that was still a long way off. "How do you feel about roots?"

"Roots?" she parroted, eyebrows furrowing as she stared at him as if he were speaking a foreign language.

"Tree roots," he clarified, eying the large, winding pieces that dipped in and out of the ground. There were a few of the older, larger trees that boasted roots large enough for her to fit between. She was small enough... where many of those that would be most likely to catch up with them first would not be. It would, perhaps, buy him enough time to get back to her before anything could go too far awry.

"To eat?" she asked, confusion and disbelief battling a muted sort of repugnance in equal parts.

His gaze swung back to her in surprise, eyebrows half lifting in question as to how she had come to that conclusion before he caught on to the way that she was following their conversation. He had mentioned food, no doubt with how hungry she was her mind kept circling back to it again. "For you to sleep in while I get you food," he corrected gently, nodding to those contorted systems of root off to the side in example.

"Oh," she breathed out, eyes following the line of his and exhaling slightly. "Okay... I can... yeah," she muttered, nodding weakly as she pushed her hands back into the earth again. Horas twitched as she stood back up once more, swaying back and forth lightly in order to keep her balance. She headed towards that nearest, largest tree as if in a stupor, stopping halfway and whirling suddenly around with wide eyes. "You won't go far?" she asked, but it sounded like more of a plea.

His head dipped, blinking slowly as he fought that urge to approach her. He was doing a lot of that now, fighting urges. Instead he just nodded. "Not far enough that I can't hear you," he assured her, watching as that tension drained from her shoulders with his words. Their bond was solidifying, whether she could feel it or not… the markers were there, the signs evident… and yet…

She didn't ask anything else, or remark on anything either, slowly moving the rest of the way to the tree, her body bending and shifting in order to try and fit through those small openings. It was a slow process, and despite how lethargic her movements, jilting and jerking weakly in a way that only seemed to cause it to stretch out longer- Horas couldn't force his feet to move.

He couldn't leave her until he had seen her actually fit inside of those roots… which, after a handful of minutes, she finally did.

He could feel his own chest easing, that worry not quite fading, but at least lessening enough that he could allow his body to drop, from two legs to four as he went off in search of that meat he had promised her.

Chapter 5

Mabry didn't even think about how hard the ground was. She didn't spend any time missing her bed or lamenting the lack of pillows. She had crawled through the root system as he had suggested and the next thing she knew she was asleep. Everything faded; the nightmare of her being kidnapped, the supernatural world she had accidentally stumbled upon, all of it. There was only the black of the back of her eyelids and the trust that Horas would keep her safe and stay within hearing distance as he had promised.

She had no real reason to trust that he would, but she did. He had gotten her out of that cage, had carried her this entire way so far, and was now worrying about her eating. Something niggled at the base of her mind, a thought not quite formed enough to examine yet, but it translated quickly into a kaleidoscope of colored, abstract dreams.

She didn't even know for sure how long she slept, or what woke her first. She was sleeping… and then there was something, whisper soft and warm against the top of her cheekbone, tracing the bone in it's curvature down. She exhaled, turning into the familiar, soothing warmth without question, her face nuzzling it like she had her pillow so many Saturday mornings after being allowed to sleep in…

But what she nuzzled was more firm than her pillow, forcing her mind to accept a more semi-conscious state, her brain grappling with her other senses as they all filtered back in one by one. Her body froze, eyes opening slowly to look first at that hand that was curved so near her face. Scar covered, bronzed knuckles rested just against the lower point of her jaw where they had stopped, his hand curled. She should have been afraid, except even without following that arm she knew whose fingers they belonged to if only for the safety she felt with him touching her.

He was back- and with him came a fragrant, rich smell of food, assaulting her sense of smell all at once as she sat bolt upright, scrambling out from between those tree limbs and past Horas where he had been crouched next to them to wake her.

A pile of logs and ashes smoldered a few feet off, the smoke from it only very small plumes that disappeared before they even made it up very far. Sand covered the top of what had once been a fire- and that smell was faint, though she didn't know how. It was the smell of what had been over the fire that drew her though.

He cooked for me.

Seared meat sat in pieces, her body almost tumbling over top of itself as she crawled rapidly towards it. Her knees almost hit her elbows when she stopped, hunching over the makeshift plate he had made from her and shoving the thickest piece of meat in her mouth. It was like heaven, the warm juices running down her chin as her teeth tore into it. She couldn't even care that when she pulled back the meat was as red as it was, or that a good deal of what was running down her chin was a pinkish-red.

It was food, and she was starving. She hadn't known it was possible to be as hungry as she was, only half aware of her body lifting slowly to sit with her legs crossed in front of her even if she was still half-hunched over the meat. She didn't even look up when she felt that body cross nearer to her again, Horas coming to sit beside her with his own meat.

It was largely quiet as they ate, outside of the noise of her scarfing her meat down, and she could feel it. Feel Horas. Even while eating it was difficult to not notice, the very air crackling between the two of them as he added slices of meat from his makeshift plate onto her own. She wanted to stop and thank him for it, for him having cooked it in the first place and him offering her the larger share, but she couldn't seem to stop pushing the meat into her mouth long enough to do so.

Each time her meat was almost diminished, his fingers would flash again, more meat appearing to her pile, until suddenly there was nothing left on either of their plates. Without thinking about it she lifted her hands, licking that juice and blood from where it had gathered over the course of her eating and only stopping once it mentally connected what she was doing. "Oh," she sighed, dropping her hands in chargrain and glancing down.

"Tell me the hunger goes away," she muttered after an uncomfortable minute, her stomach rumbling even though she was sure she had eaten more than what should have been enough to satisfy her.

Horas snorted in amusement, yellow eyes taking her in kindly and without apparent judgment even with how self-conscious she suddenly was. "No," he bluntly answered, setting his plate off to the side and leaning forward somewhat, elbows pressing into his knees. "It doesn't. You just adjust. Right now it's just worse because you are so close to the first shift."

Mabry's heart dropped, stomach clenching at his admittance. She couldn't imagine staying this hungry forever, or imagine how it was that she would manage such a state either. She stilled entirely, wide eyes flashing up to his as he leant even further forward, his thumb brushing along the side of her lips and gathering the blood and juice that she had left there to wipe it down off of her face entirely.

Her heart hammered in her chest, skin heating in the path that his thumb had made and her muscles tensing. It didn't… feel bad, and she thought that maybe that scared her more than if it would have. Her eyes dropped again, trying to hide the blush that burned from her neck up as she tried to remember what she had been going to say before he touched her like that.

"In the movies it always seems like it hurts," she finally said after a long moment, statement more of a question than anything, but when he didn't answer right away she finally forced herself to lift her gaze again. "That's probably just stupid Hollywood stuff right?" she asked, her tone a guarded kind of hopefully optimistic.

His eyes are just so pretty…

The varying shades of yellow that made up his irises seemed to whirl as she stared at him, getting caught in the neon refraction. *He was just so pretty*. His hair was longer than she usually preferred, his skin that deep bronze that only came from a lot of time under the sun… Even his scars seemed wild though, not nearly as numerous as those from the pack they had just run from, but still abundantly covered, the paler flesh crisscrossing in some places. It was the yellow of his eyes though- and the way that he looked at her that had her heart racing, even sitting so still as they were.

"Did it hurt for you?" she probed, her nerves betraying her by entering into her voice beneath that last word.

She watched Horas' eyes shift again, that intensity he had been regarding her with only reducing the barest amount as he shrugged. "Depends on the person," he explained, running a blade of grass gently between his thumb and forefinger. "For some people the first shift doesn't hurt at all. The first one I changed… his hurt," his eyes took on a distant look, voice dropping somewhat as he focused on whatever he was internalizing. "Bad. For a while."

Maybry swallowed, surprised at how shocked she was to hear that he had turned anyone, much less the faint trace of jealousy that came with it. *That was just ridiculous.*

She didn't want to change in the first place, so to be jealous that it had to someone else was insane.

"He got used to it after the first few times," Horas continued, eyes coming back more fully to her with a wry sort of smile, as if to acknowledge his momentary absence. "Mine? Not so much. But then, I was a born wolf, not changed. I don't know if that makes a difference or not." He trailed off, his eyes flicking down from her face to her shoulder.

Mabry took a moment longer to understand what he was looking at, eyes glancing down to catch sight of that bite mark that stood out so glaringly against her fair skin. It took her another long moment for her to realize that his hand had moved back to her again. His thumb didn't move for more leftover juice and blood this time, but instead moved to the still jagged, unhealed marks by her clavicle where the woman's teeth had torn her flesh.

Her mouth dried, moving from watching the way that his fingers probed around the edge of it instead to his face, watching the play of emotion that took place there as he looked at her bite mark. She didn't know what to make of that anger. Nor did she know what to make of that other more elusive, darker emotion that lurked behind it. So instead she cleared her throat.

"I'm scared," she admitted quietly, words almost a whisper and dying out as his eyes shot up to meet hers, his thumb just barely brushing over the center of her mark. He almost looked apologetic and that was enough for her to sink into the contact, relaxing into their conversation somewhat. "How many have you changed?" she asked, curiosity getting the better of her.

"Two," he answered in that stilted way that she was beginning to realize was a form of his discomfort. "Only two," he clarified, eyes moving slowly back to her mark and allowing his thumb to depress that skin somewhat- as if testing it.

Mabry winced, that sharp burn of discomfort from the action sudden and unwelcome. However, when she went to pull back from it she felt his hand over her shoulder tighten, holding her in place and having her meet his eyes more fully again. Her breath stuttered from her lips as she stared at him, uncertain as to what that look on his face actually meant but finding her body responding in all too inappropriate ways for it regardless. Her thighs shifted, eyes widening as his nostrils flared.

He absolutely can not smell me right now, I'm imagining that!

She shifted again, uncomfortable laughter filtering out of her as she shrugged. "I've never been great with pain," she offered awkwardly as a subject change. Her eyes broke from his once more, looking down to his hand and where it rest on her shoulder. "I broke my ankle when I was thirteen and I put up such a fight in the doctor's office they ended up putting me out in order to reset it," Mabry babbled, piling her words on top of one another frantically.

Flirting came naturally to her, it was what had gotten her into this whole mess… but something felt different, her chest tight, just from having Horas touch her like he was. It felt good, but not in the way that she was used to attention feeling, and that made her so uncomfortable she felt like she was close to coming right out of her skin.

"Thank you for saving me," she blurted, at such odds with her emotions and the way that they were shifting so quickly within her that she didn't know how to stem the words in her mouth. Not even when he looked at her like he was now, a shifting of emotions on his own features that made her want to ask even more questions.

"Don't thank me yet," he said after a short pause, looking back over his shoulder as if checking their surroundings once before shrugging. "If they catch us, it will be worse, like I said… Right now we are just lucky to be far enough ahead." Horas trailed off again, his nostrils flaring, scenting the air close to her as if searching for something before lifting his hand to his mouth, forefinger and thumb pushing between his lips momentarily.

Mabry watched, entranced, as he moved his hand back to her, smoothing that saliva covered skin over her mark slowly, rounding out the edges as if he were smoothing lotion over her instead of his spit. She should have been repulsed. She should have been outraged, something. Anything other than that strange flipping sensation she got in her lower belly, lips opening only far enough for her own tongue to wet the line of them hesitantly. "What are you doing?"

"Taking her smell off of you," Horas answered without so much as looking up from what he was doing. His gaze was focused, nostrils wrinkling at the mention of that other wolf's smell, and a very large part of her was secretly pleased with that. "You smell better on your own," he muttered, as if unaware he had even mentioned it.

"I smell like her?" she asked dumbly, blinking at the thought of it. She hadn't ever really considered what she must smell like to them, and the more she thought about it the more uncomfortable she suddenly felt. She couldn't remember the last time she had been able to shower and she was covered still in remnants of blood, dirt from that cage, and who knew what else.

A crazy, biting Alpha-bitch, apparently.

"It's in where she bit you," he explained, fingers testing that ragged skin again. "Her scent carried through her saliva," his head lifted suddenly, without warning, his eyes flashing in the orange and red glow of the evening. "I could bite over it, if you'd like, but then you would be carrying my scent." His words came so much faster than the ones before, intensity of his gaze burning straight through her and into the pit of her belly.

It was such a mix of emotions, her reactions to what he was suggesting… Biting her again sounded painful, especially with the memory of the one on her shoulder being so recent… but at the same time her body was responding to the suggestion, back arching as if to push herself closer to him despite her not trying to consciously do so. "Uh-" she stuttered out, her body heating.

"I wouldn't force you," he assured her empathetically, pulling back somewhat with obvious concern written into his features. "It was just an offer. To get her scent off of you… Would make it easier to run…" he stopped, flinching, his body tensing somewhat as he sighed. She wanted to question it but his eyes broke from hers, lifting to the trees above them in obvious frustration.

"That's a lie," he confessed, words stiff. "They would still have our scent to track." His gaze dropped back to hers more slowly, lips parting and that same intense expression filtering back into his features and voice. His tongue pressed into his lower lip, tracing that firm line and forcing her eyes there too. "I just want to bite you," he admitted, obvious growl beneath the words.

And it hit her like a freight train. What that look that his face had taken meant, the extra emphasis around the word bite… it was sexual. The act, at least how he was talking about it, was very obviously sexual, her eyes lifting from his lips to his eyes and dropping again as she crossed her thighs closer together.

She didn't have the words for him then, breath rushing out as she licked her lips. What he was saying… was affecting her, and obviously so, heart hammering and her skin breaking out in what felt like a heat rash. Suddenly all she wanted was his hands on her, the both of them, taking her with the possessive urgency that his voice had dropped to with his last sentence. It was just the memory of her last bite that was stopping her, clinging to the edges of her memory and only just keeping her from throwing her body across that space between them and fully at him.

Chapter 6

Horas' whole body felt like it was on edge, watching her lick her lips like she was now, her gaze skittering from his own and down again repeatedly like a deer caught in the headlights. He had been scenting it on her for the better part of their conversation now, that heavy attraction that she kept dancing around. Smelling her and those ever revolving emotions as her heartbeat sang within her ribcage, daring him to urge it faster.

It was maddening, keeping himself in line. He had been reminding himself over and over that now wasn't the time, that they at least needed to make it another few days ahead before he broached anything with her, but looking at her now was testing those limits… Especially with the way she wasn't refusing his offer to bite her.

He wasn't sure he had any patience left. He knew what was prudent, he knew the risks, but the way that her body was unconsciously leaning towards him, the scent of her arousal wafting from between her thighs like it was, and the way that her eyes kept flickering about him- his limits were all but gone.

"Oh?" Mabry echoed, voice a breathy kind of surprised, the scent of her arousal battling with that of her anxiety. She had no idea that she was the one in control of this now, that she held the reigns, and that made her all the more sexy for it. Her neck tilted, twisting just enough to the side to allow his thumb where it still brushed along her mark more access. "Would it hurt the same?"

Her words were barely more than air, chest rising and falling with her suddenly deep breaths. Horas' own lips shifted at the sight of it, breaking apart into a rakish grin as his fingers adjusted their angle, his thumb moving instead to brush along just under her jawline. "No," he promised her seriously, even with the evidence of his desire grating his tone. "Doesn't have to hurt. She was sloppy and careless."

She had attacked Mabry in the heat of the moment, rushing her with no finesse or build-up. Even though the pain was always going to be a factor, there were ways around it... ways to distract that body so that the pain was the least of its focus. What he was promising her was so very different from that brutal assault of her person that had happened the night she was taken.

For her part, Mabry seemed to understand that, and in the pause after his words he could see her trusting it as well, her anxiety lessening the more that desire took over, a soft sigh escaping her only in that moment before she leant the rest of the way forward, pushing to her knees in order to put her body in close enough proximity to his. Her green eyes were hooded, her hands hesitantly coming to his shoulders.

It was all of the permission that he needed.

Without another word his body shifted to match, pulling her face to him and slanting his lips over hers warmly. There was none of the hesitation their words had carried, none of the question there. She fit against him like a glove, adhering to the harsher contours of his body even as he tilted her chin back.

Where they had questions- the physicality between them was indisputable. The bond that he had been fighting was so much more enduring than their fleeting understanding. Her lips opened under his willingly, a shuddered sigh passing from her body to his as she gave herself into it. He could feel her accepting that bond, her body pushing up further into his even as he worked to lower her body down to her back on the earth behind them.

It was a task she didn't even attempt to fight him in. Her hands were rushed, pushing against the thin shirt on his torso as of trying to remove it by that alone, her tongue pressing against the entrance of his mouth needily, frantically. It was like she was afraid they would be interrupted at any moment.

Because of that his movements were slower, more sure, tongue meeting hers hungrily and pulling it into his mouth as he lowered her, fitting himself between her thighs and lowering his torso down fully onto the softness of hers. He could feel each gasping breath she drew, the way that her back arched against that ground to try and push herself closer to him.

He broke from her lips softly, trailing his own down the line of her jaw and towards her neck. "Careful, girl," he growled into the shell of her ear, pushing his hips between the juncture of her legs again to feel her thighs lift off of the ground to meet him. "I'm in no rush."

Mabry's answering moan was plaintive, staccato rhythm of her heartbeat pattering against his lips as he ran them down her neck, tasting that skin there- tasting the way that her desperation transferred between their two bodies. "I told you I have no intention of being either sloppy or careless." Not for his marking of her. He wanted to bend her body in half and drag her inside out, leaving every inch between there and the next point covered in his scent so deeply that one wouldn't be able to tell where she ended and he began.

The rotating tint of the setting sun played over their bodies, filtered between the leaves of the trees as he finally allowed his hands the access to roam down her sides, tracing those subtle curves with heavy reverence. He wasn't kidding about being in no rush, he didn't cheat and run his hands anywhere but her sides, revelling in the way that her body arched and shook with even just that little of contact. It was only when his fingers met the hem of her shirt that he shifted his grip, lifting her shirt just enough to fit his palms beneath so that as he drug them back up the same route of her body that they had gone down, her shirt was forced to lift with it.

He had every intention of taking his time. Ideally he would have had an unlimited amount of it to do as he wished. Ideally he would have had even more time to work her up into a real frenzy, his touches light and his mouth heavy, but he knew that they were on borrowed time here. As much as he wanted to forget about that pursuing force entirely, he couldn't allow himself to. Nor could he fight taking what it was she was so freely offering any longer.

His palms pressed into her skin, running up and over the center of her flesh until the smooth plains of her stomach met those rounded protrusions of her chest. She was, by no means, extraordinarily large breasted, but with her nipples pushing into the centers of his palms she fit near perfectly within his large hands. His fingers flexed, trying that flesh and the flexibility of it as her nipples hardened into firm beaks inside of his grasp.

What had been a low growl worked its way into a groan, his thumbs sweeping the undersides of her breasts in order to find that pebbled flesh in their center and rub against it instead. The breathy, enraptured moan that he received in return was almost enough to make him forget his goal. He needed her distracted, he needed her so overcome with her need that she was near bursting from her skin.

"Can you feel that?" he asked her, his hunger deepening his tone even as he pinched his thumb to his palm, with her nipples still trapped between. She gasped, back coming off of the ground and her thighs shuddering from where they wrapped around his hips instinctively. "Your body is swelling," he groaned into her neck, tracing that vein down it and nearly growling again as her scent ripened further.

"Making itself ready for me," it was like a praise and a revelation at once as it left his lips, dragging her shirt up and over her head to be discarded without another thought, leaving her bare before his eyes. Her chest was heaving, that pretty eruption of crimson flushing upwards against freckles that he hadn't even expected to find there. Her nipples were a darker coral color, as rigid as the rest of her was soft, tightening under his glance alone.

He didn't have the words for her, his accolades transforming into a deep, rumbling series of groans as he lowered his head, lips capturing the stiffened peak of one breast even as his thumbs worked to undo the buttons above her pelvis. Her hands moved from his shoulders to his hair, tangling about the curls in his hair as if trying to hold him where he stayed. But it was the noises leaving her lips that caught him, loud and without any filter on them, her moans tumbling about the treeline and reverberating back to him.

"Please- God, Horas," she panted, hips rotating as if trying to help him in ridding her of her pants even as one hand drifted back down, her nails catching at the shoulder of his shirt. Her impatience took hold, body shaking as those nails curved down and the seams of his shirt ripped in response, a throaty laugh leaving him at the feel of the air cooling his overheated back.

"Ask me nicer," he hummed, pushing her jeans off of her hips and allowing her squirming legs to do the rest of the work even as he worked at getting his own jeans down with one hand. "Beg me pretty," he muttered, tone caught somewhere between a demand and a plea himself as he finished with his pants and moved his hand to her thigh.

"I don't-" Mabry breathed out, words trembling into moan as his palm ran up the inside of her, fingers finding that moist center and parting her folds even as his thumb sought out that more sensitive bundle at the top of them. "Oh, please, Horas," she begged. "I want to feel you. I need you. Please." Her words tumbled seemingly unbidden, gasped out of her as he fit two fingers inside of her, working them into a pulsating rhythm opposite the circular one his thumb had found.

He had wanted to take it slow, but that was nearing impossible, the way that her body called to his. His lips lifted, finding purchase against hers again as her hips lifted into each stroke of his fingers, succession of moans and gasps matching that rhythm easily. He was just going to have to-

All thought cut off as her questing hands found him, wrapping about his dick and rolling her fingers over the hardened surface of his head. His hips jutted instinctively into the pull of her fingers, long moan filtering out of his lips and into the parting of hers with as much need as her hips were displaying. Without pause he broke away from her once more, removing his fingers despite her breathy protestations and instead grabbing her hips.

It was rushed and deprived, his eyes flashing against the gathering darkness as he flipped her, hands holding her hips and lifting them from the ground where the front of her body had fallen. "Please what?" he demanded darkly, growl filling each syllable as he lifted her ass into the air, positioning himself right at the wet, open center of her with the last vestiges of his iron control.

"Please, Horas, please- fuck me," she pleaded, face turning into the side of the dirt and her hips pushing back against his grip in wanton desperation.

Desperation that he readily met with her words, pushing forward until he could feel himself disappearing inside of her, a kind of all encompassing need taking over his very thrusts. "Fuck," he rasped out, the bond between them shaking with the force of their physical connection. He could feel it- building beneath his skin like the force of the universe was demanding it, demanding this. He could feel her breath, rising in pitch to meet his own, the way that her internal muscles clamped around him with the sensation of their connection.

Raw and visceral, his body bowed, thumb finding her clit again to aid in the tremors he could feel building beneath her muscles, begging her body to give into what he demanded of it-

And Gods, did she.

She pushed her shoulders further into the ground, meeting him thrust for thrust as her body trembled to pieces beneath him, her voice a long low wail of praise and delight for the orgasm that shook her. The one that he was encouraging to continue, thumb rolling against her slick skin as he nuzzled her face further to the side, lips brushing reverently over the mark from that other… and his teeth closing suddenly and without warning over it, pushing his own scent into place overtop it.

Her scream was equal parts pain and pleasure, head thrown back as he fell into her, his own climax overtaking him.

Chapter 7

Mabry didn't have words.

Her mind was a kaleidoscope of emotion and color flashing behind her closed lids, body limp beneath the larger, warmer one that still lay over it. She could still feel where his teeth had rebroken her skin, but unlike before there was a warmth with it. Painful but not. She didn't know how to explain it even to herself, moaning in disappointment when he pulled out of her more fully and rolled off to the side.

I don't need to breathe.

She wanted to assure him of as much, to promise him that he could roll back and crush her and she would be fine, but her throat was raw, her voice nonexistent in those moments following how thoroughly he had claimed her. It was like everything in the world had just suddenly… righted itself, all of the negativity and fear from the past few days disappearing in the wake of his body atop hers.

She shifted, a rush of energy forcing her to push her hands up under herself, lifting until she was on her hands and knees and suddenly freezing. Something within her felt… off. Her body heating even further despite the slowing of the desire that had been seizing her so. Her heartbeat hammered faster and faster, speeding until she felt it would really burst entirely from her chest. "I don't," she started, her voice hewn with the fear and sudden anxiety that seized her. She didn't get any more words out though.

From beside her she could feel Horas, sitting up and his hand firm between her shoulder blades. "Stop fighting it," he commanded her, voice a sure sort of stern that only made her want to ask him more questions, but it was like his demand released something within her. Her chest hollowed, air rushing from her all at once as she half-fell forward, her fingers digging into the hard earth.

A long, low groan filtered of her lips as they pulled back from her teeth, eyes flashing as something burned low in her abdomen. Her bones stretched, pushing and twisting in on themselves and she could feel it. All at once. Like they were breaking inside of themselves, fissures working along each of them in millions of turns, a rapid fire cracking and breaking of bone and skin, her back arching and…

Oh, God, that was fur.

Pale red, brilliant in hue, where her fingers had been claws struck dirt instead, large paws grinding against the earth as her mind spun, trying to come to terms with what she was seeing, with what she was feeling. There was no way it had happened that fast. But it had. She could feel it. Coursing within her, within this new body that felt so similar yet opposite her own that she was used to. Her lips opened again, a low, reedy whine whittling its way out-

And then she collapsed.

Her eyes widened, shocked to see fur melding back to skin, to see her body shifting and shrinking before her very eyes. For a long moment she just lay there, staring at her very human hands in front of her face, saying nothing. For a long moment Horas let her.

"Did I just-" she stuttered out, surprised to hear words and not barking, her eyes lifting up to his and blinking widely. And again when she caught sight of his eyes, blinking hard at how much more in focus the whole of him suddenly was. She had thought he was handsome, but this, this was otherworldly. He was beautiful. How had she missed all of those scars on his face?

How had she missed the scar that broke between his left eyebrow and carried almost down all the way to his eyelid? His eyes weren't just yellow, as she had thought previously, but a burnt umber color flecked with gold. It was like she was looking at a different person entirely, lips parting and a soft sigh breaking from her.

And his smell...

Like old leather and a fresh spring morning, the faintest trace of cinnamon rounding it out... She wanted to lick him all over again, crawl her way into his lap and force him to hold her. She almost did, but the world was coming back into focus too sharply, and the way that he was laughing was making her freeze. It was like seeing everything for the first time, like what Becky had described it like when she had first gotten contacts...

There were more colors, more details, more of everything.

"That," Horas rumbled, a pleased sort of amused as he took over for her, pulling her body between his thighs and wrapping his arms around her waist as he nuzzled her neck. "Was your first turn Mabry." He sounded inordinately proud, and with that sound there was a smell, like a deepening of his own, but with a crisp edge that smelt like... he was pleased? How did emotions have smells? And how was she supposed to know which was which?

"It happened so fast..." she muttered, eyes cutting to him in obvious question. She had been expecting to change on the first full moon following her being bitten. She had been expecting to be a wolf all night and to run around until sun up, chasing her own tail or biting fleas, or some other such nonsense. Not just flashing into one skin and then the next…

"It was your first turn," he soothed, palms rubbing up and down either arm comfortingly, warming her back up and encouraging her back to sink into his chest trustingly. "I told you, it's different for everyone. Sometimes its minutes, sometimes its days," he broke off, chuckling again as she flinched at the days.

She supposed, put into perspective like that, she would have preferred it this way rather than days.

She still shifted somewhat though, feeling his lips against her neck and wanting to allow it to continue. "I swear," she muttered, closing her eyes and giving into those new sensations. "It's almost like I can feel you now… how *weird* is that?"

Horas snorted at her throat, amusement clear in both scent and tone as he shrugged. "You probably can," he admitted, his lips pushing into a smile against her shoulder and making her own lips shift upwards in return even without being able to see him. She wanted to see him smile. She had only been allowed to witness it a few short times in the time she had known him and even those had seemed special.

"So wolves can just feel one another?!" she demanded, eyebrows raising and her mind whirring with the possibilities in that. Did that mean she was going to be able to feel that other pack? Would they be able to feel her? Envy worked up alongside that worried curiosity, suddenly possessive about anyone else, wolf or not, being able to feel Horas like that.

He snorted again, one hand lifting to push her blonde hair out of the way and off to one side. "Not every wolf," he half-laughed, kissing up the side of one shoulder towards her neck, "just mates."

She could feel him freeze even just after he had said it, his body tensing in time with hers and his breath catching behind her in his throat. The word hung like a fog in the clearing, repeating in her head with clearer intent each time. *Mates*.

"Mates?" she echoed, her voice monotone and her stomach dropping as she pushed his hands, wiggling out from under his hold and scrambling away from him on her knees until she was far enough to turn around and face him. She might have assumed that it was just the word he was using since they had just had sex… but the way that he had frozen… "What does that mean?" she demanded, an icy chill forcing goosebumps along her arms as she watched his face lose the last of that brevity that it had held moments before.

"Fuck, I -" he cut off, hand lifting to jerkily push through the curls of his hair with an aggravated pinch to his features. His scent was more bitter then, pervading her nostrils and forcing them to flare as her eyes narrowed. "I didn't want to explain it like this," he admitted haltingly, eyes flashing as they lifted to meet her gaze once more.

"What. Does. Mates. Mean. Horas?" she bit out, rage crawling up the back of her throat and all of the emotion that had earlier softened her muscles evaporating from her.

"It's when you find your mate. It's pretty self explanatory," he muttered, lips thinning as he broke her gaze once more to look upwards in that way it seemed he managed when uncomfortable with the topic being discussed. Like he couldn't quite meet her gaze.

"How do you know?"

His shoulders tensed at the cutting edge to her tone, his own eyes narrowing somewhat as he took in her defensive stance. "It's their scent," he offered after a short pause, one shoulder lifting. "It's a feeling, you just know."

"And wolves can only be mated to wolves?" she continued, her head spinning as she sought any way out of the sudden betrayal that she felt with his words. Like she had been mislead… or like he was lying to her. She didn't know which, but both left her feeling hollow and cold after what they had just shared.

What if he really did just want me to mate with? What if this was all some sick, twisted game?

"Not necessarily," he hedged, chin dropping as he blew out a frustrated sigh, shrugging his shoulders and gesturing irritatedly with one hand. "It is generally how it ends up. The urge to turn your mate tends to be too strong and not many want to face the inevitably shorter lifespan of their mate remaining human…"

"But you can have a mate who is human?" she verified, voice raising a half octave after she asked, because the look on his face told her that she had guessed it right, that it was possible, and her sudden bursting of her body off of her knees and to her feet sprang dirt in multiple directions. "So you've known! This whole time!" She accused, the betrayal finally seeping down into her bones and grabbing hold of the very center of her being…

"If you're even telling me the truth!" she yelled, backing away from him further as he lifted to his own feet, hand lifted as if to placate her, but she didn't want to hear it. "No! Don't! You didn't say *anything to me* back when I was in that cage about this. You didn't say anything before now… How am I supposed to know that you didn't just take the opportunity presented to you and trick me into all of this?! How am I supposed to-"

Mabry cut off suddenly, a howl overtaking the last of her words from somewhere not too far off, and her whole body stilled in its entirety, eyes flashing as she turned back to Horas, fear filtering over anything and everything else.

Chapter 8

That howl rent through the night air like a siren, Horas' hair standing on end the moment that it sounded. It was too close, too sudden, and he had been so lost in Mabry that he had allowed the bearer of it to sneak up on them. His eyes flashed back to her newly yellowed ones, snarl breaking over his features as he jerked his head in the opposite direction. "Run!" he yelled, planting his feet in the ground beneath him.

He could give her a head start, at the very least. Just because it only sounded like one wolf didn't mean that more weren't coming.

But Mabry wasn't running, her fear-filled eyes centered on him as she backed into the tree behind her, her fingers ripping at the bark as she shook her head. Damnit. It was the wrong time for her to be sentimental, hadn't she just accused him of being one of them?! Even if he knew where she had been coming from, even though he understood it was everything compiled all at once, he wished that she would hold to that belief even if only as long as it took for her to run.

"Dammit girl," he cursed, half-turning towards her to try and spur her into action when that body came flying out of the treeline to his right. Black fur and snarling jowls, it's teeth caught his shoulder, dragging him down to the ground with a sickening crunch of bone and tearing flesh. His answering grunt was full of pain, but the way that his body shifted was not.

He didn't pause, or wait for those teeth to leave him before he shifted, even knowing that it would make the injury of that shoulder worse, he allowed fur to grow in place of skin and his body to grow. With a howl of his own he spun on the creature flanking him, paw smashing against the side of its face as it gave up purchase of his shoulder in pursuit of his jaw, and sending it flying a few steps back.

Just enough for him to work his body between she and Mabry with a menacing growl, sinking down just enough that he was prepared to launch up and off the ground at her should she move any closer. But it seemed the person that they had sent was smarter than that, the black wolf pacing a few steps back and eyeing both he and Mabry speculatively.

Tension held the both of their bodies stiff and he was more surprised than upset when she rose to her back legs, olive-hued flesh replacing that black fur slowly.

Sasha.

Her black hair hung in soft waves down her bare shoulders, orange-flecked eyes flashing as she lifted her chin to better look at them. She was beautiful, even with the new mass of scars that her body hosted, and her imperious gaze was nonetheless intimidating for it. Alpha. He had known that it was she who had bit Mabry, but he never expected her to pursue them on her own.

"If you wanted a turn with the human, Horas, all you had to do was ask… Not steal her away in the midst of our celebration," Sasha greeted, narrowed gaze moving over his still turned form before flicking to Mabry behind him as if she were no more than an annoying spectator. He knew that she had to smell the Change on Mabry, just as he knew that her stopping and speaking at all was the one and only chance she would give them at a resolution to this debacle absent a fight…

So he raised himself to two feet as well, ignoring the sharp gasp behind him and refusing to move from his stance in front of Mabry. "She's no longer human," he responded evenly, careful to keep that aggravation from bleeding into his tone as he felt a warm, small hand travel up his back from where Mabry had walked to peer out from behind him.

"That changes very little," Sasha answered with a sneer, shaking her head as she continued to ignore Mabry. "She was one of ours, taken by our pack, by law she should have remained with us… And yet you spirited her away into the dead of morning, and *lay* with her?"

Horas could feel Mabry's indignation building from behind him, but his arm twisted only enough to touch his hand to the one now at his side, holding it for a moment to keep her from interrupting. "She's mine," he asserted composedly, ignoring that shock and anger that bled off of the alpha in front of him at those words. "My mate. By our laws my right supercedes yours." Even if he had mishandled it and gone out of order, he knew that much to still be true.

Sasha laughed though, a cold, savage thing at his words. If anything, hearing them only flinted her gaze further. "And what proof have you to back these claims Horas?" she demanded, one ebony brow raising high on her forehead as she surveyed the pair of them stonily. He needed no proof, and they both knew that, but he also knew that she had little desire to give up what she had found as a solution for her pack's problems.

"Is my word not enough?"

"She's ours. I found her, I changed her. You let her come back to the pack and bear us pups and we will allow you to come with her," Sasha offered dismissively, one shoulder rolling in a shrug as if it didn't matter to her. As if what she was offering was a deal that Horas couldn't afford to pass up.

"You will find others," Horas defended, shaking his head. "Your pack used to boast many more females than it does now, it can again. But my mate will not be one of them." He could feel Mabry at his back, her nails digging into the skin there at just the thought of going back, and he could offer her no words of assurance that he wouldn't let that happen, not here, not now.

Sasha grimaced, throwing her hair back over one shoulder. "We've no need of more females. Just the one. She will do. Maybe one or two more like her, disposable… I don't need any other competitors in my pack, that's why they've all been done away with. This one here, she's pretty enough for them to whelp off of, but human- and a captive, and so she will never be allowed to rise in rank." She said it so calmly, her eyes moving to Mabry as if surveying her again to ensure herself of what she said.

Her words were shocking on their own though, Horas' mind instantly going to reject what it was that she was suggesting, but she had put it so plainly...

"Do you think I'll be replaced? That I'll allow myself to risk losing my position to some new female?" Sasha laughed, incredulity creeping into her tone. "No, I chose this one for so many reasons... her family whelps boys, not her mother, but then genetically I've been assured she's more likely to take after her father. I don't need females coming into my pack by any means. We grow in number and we repeat the process. If you will not hand her back Horas..." she trailed off, her threat clear in her words as she cut her gaze back to him.

For his part, all Horas could do was stare, bewilderment pulling the corners of his eyes. No matter what she was saying now, females weren't what determined the sex of a child- genetic predisposition or not. And further, what she was saying made it seem a whole lot less like Mabry had been chosen in the heat of the moment, at random...

And more like Sasha had stalked and chosen her...

"You can't-" he began, that disbelief clear in his words as he spoke, and cutting off as Sasha lunged. Apparently her patience was depleted, her movement only giving him enough time to throw Mabry from directly behind his back and shove himself forward to meet Sasha head on.

She didn't bother turning, or trying to take their fight back to four legs, her claws reached out from human hands, slashing at his neck even as he grappled with her. Sasha was, in many ways, his superior. Her body was quick and agile, claws slashing where her teeth snapped, body dipping and bending around his as if she were going to catch a weak spot.

She had far more training in the art of fighting than he did, far more experience to have earned herself twice the amount of scars he held with the pack that she led. She was war and violence breathed into a an already ferocious she-wolf.

And she wasn't trying to lose her one and only brood-mare this easily.

Her hand struck against his shoulder, claws cutting through the skin there and down, dragging and ripping it with a snarl even as he tried to counter it- but his movements were slower than hers, his attention diverted…

And the moment that she sunk her teeth into his neck it seemed as if the whole forest went quiet, blood spurting from around the edges of her mouth as she growled- and a scream behind them tore the air like a high-pitched alarm bell.

Chapter 9

Mabry didn't feel as if she were in control of her own body.

Everything from the past few days just kept fluctuating so quickly it was like she was never given enough time to catch up and figure out where she was actually standing. She had been upset with Horas, and a very real part of her wanted to remain so, but with the alpha that had turned her standing there it had been all that Mabry could do not to scream for Horas to run with her.

It wasn't just a safety thing any longer, even without the sex, even with her questioning what he said and his motives for not telling her… She knew that he had to be telling the truth because she could feel it. Like his heartbeat was in line with hers, as if they beat with a sacred synchronicity. Seeing that scarred, terrifying wolf facing him down had only made it more apparent.

She didn't want to see Horas hurt.

She didn't want to see him fighting even, her heart in her throat as she watched the woman jump at him, still human in form, and sink her teeth into his neck in a move that looked all too familiar, despite her never having seen it herself. She could still feel it, the way that those teeth had torn her flesh and ripped her apart so viciously that the pain had ingrained itself into her very muscles.

Except when Sasha had bitten Mabry it had been closer to her shoulder- and the area she bit Horas in was higher, more dangerous, the blood that gushed from the impact enough for Mabry's lips to open, her shrill, terror-filled scream pulsating out of her throat and into the forest at the sight. "No!" she screamed, jumping forward without thinking further on the motion. Or the repercussions for her doing so.

Suddenly what had happened to her didn't matter. How she had come to meet Horas- didn't matter. All that mattered was that Horas continue breathing, that the bitch whose teeth were pushing through his flesh release her hold.

She flew at the pair of them, her entire body shaking as a foreign, low-pitched growl vibrated out of her bared teeth. Sasha's amber eyes flicking to her just moments before her mouth opened, releasing her hold on Horas with a feral, bloody grin. Crimson dripped from her exposed canines and down her chin, thick clotted streams broken up only by the bits of Horas' flesh that stuck with her as Sasha growled in return.

She lunged at Mabry, but Mabry couldn't be stopped, her hands grappling inexpertly for the she-wolf's throat with a grief ridden scream.

Sasha ducked, weaving her way out of Mabry's grasp and her teeth snapping mere inches from Mabry's face. Whatever fear might have entered Mabry was cut off though by the sight of dark, curly hair rising behind the woman's frame.

What had already been a fast-paced scene seemed to speed up even further; Mabry blinking as Horas' broad, scarred hands wrapped around Sasha's throat from behind. The tips of his fingernails blackened even as she watched, a deep, resounding growl echoing through the space they were in as Sasha's eyes grew wide, her hands shifting to reach up to those hands about her own throat, desperate fingers clawing in an attempt to remove them from her person.

When her frantic movement yielded nothing she turned to scratching, deep red lines appearing across Horas' bronzed skin, but his grip changed not at all.

Sasha's feet lifted off the ground as Horas raised her, feet kicking idly in the air as she sputtered, spittle flying from her lips and the scent of her fear permeating the clearing in a thick, bitter cloud. Mabry couldn't look away, her lips opening as she watched, immobile.

"I said," Horas growled, his own shifting nails pricking the olive skin of Sasha's neck, little dots of blood erupting upon the surface. "Not. My. Mate." he bit out every word, his fingers sinking suddenly behind his nails, those dots of blood bursting into streams as he tore through the tendons and muscles- ripping straight through the corded muscles of her neck until her head was half-hewn from her shoulders.

Mabry watched as he dropped that body, those wild, raven waves tilting at an inhuman angle to the side, the wide orange gaze of Sasha's dead eyes locked in perpetual fear across from her at nothing.

It wasn't until Horas breathed roughly out, stumbling a few steps forward and his hand lifting to that injury on his neck that Mabry snapped back to life, a whine leaking out of her lips as she hurriedly turned to him. "Oh my God," she exhaled, the words breathy and full of fear and worry. "You-" she cut off, running at him with a suddenness that surprised even herself.

Her hands were hesitant, fluttering barely over his person, shifting from his chest and down, never quite making full contact with his skin as if afraid that she might make his pain worse. "You let her bite your neck," she whisper-wailed, her eyes flashing as she stared up at him in obvious distress.

He had almost died for her, he might still die for her.

"I-" she cut off with the way that his hand fell, that blood still obviously coating the side of his neck, but those gaping injuries she had seen before seemingly already somehow smaller. "You-" she cut off again, her breath catching in her throat as she finally allowed her palms to settle against his bloody chest.

"It's fine," he soothed, voice rough, but obviously amused. She didn't understand what he had to be amused about or why he was grinning so largely at her with so much skin missing from his throat, covered in so much of his own and Sasha's blood… She almost couldn't get things straight in her mind at all.

"It's just a bite," he continued, voice pitched low as he stepped into her, forcing her body back into that tree behind her. Her shoulder blades hit the bark behind her, reminding her of her unclothed state for the first time since before Sasha had even shown up. "It's not a big deal," he promised.

She wanted to disagree with him, to tell him that he was out of his mind, but all she could do was open her lips, a strange noise filtering out of them breathily as she felt her pupils dilate, his scent hitting her all at once and filling his nostrils.

Oh. Oh he smelled good.

"You can't just… pretend you didn't just almost die," she finally whispered, pain lacing her words in too telling of a manner. She didn't want to say the words aloud, or go back to fighting with him, not when the evidence of his desire was pressed so firmly into the tops of her thighs, reminding her of just what it felt like to have him inside and filling her.

"I'm not pretending anything," he responded, voice just as low, and even more dangerously pitched for the manner in which he sidled up in front of her, his hand coming to cup one side of her face so delicately that it almost wasn't even a caress. "I almost died. She almost kept you. And you fought to keep me alive," his words were warm, wrapping around her seductively.

"I couldn't let you die," she admitted huskily, her shaking face lifting up to him despite all of the uncertainty over everything else. She knew that to be true. "I don't know what else is happening… I don't know what any of this is, or how to be a wolf. I don't know what mates are or why you didn't tell me… but I can feel you. In my bones, in my veins. Like you're inside of me."

"Not yet I'm not," he muttered darkly, lips descending on hers with no more warning than that, his tongue claiming her mouth with heated passion. There was no build up like before, no careful consideration of her body. It was all heated need and desire, the emotions from before translated with a sensual press of skin and muscle.

Mabry moaned, the bark rubbing roughly against her nipples as he flipped her suddenly, pressing her front to the tree and lifting one of her thighs at a hard, high angle, his body sliding into her own with no more than a grind of his hips into the backs of her ass. Her hands shot out, catching around the sides of the trees as she arched back, pushing back into him and trying to encourage those movements. "I-" she cut off.

Horas' free hand shifted, fingers twisting up in her blonde hair and curling it about his wrist as he yanked her hair back to allow him access to her face with the way she was bent into the tree, hot lips trailing the line of her jaw avidly. "You?" he prompted, hips pulling back to slowly ease himself out of her.

"Oh, God, Horas," she groaned, breath catching loudly as he slammed back into her, forcing her body even more forward into the tree in front of her.

"I can't- I just- Oh, God, I love you," the words tumbled out amid a series of moans and gasps, flying from her before she could second guess or stem them- and the rough pace that his hips picked up in reward was enough to distract her from just what she had said. He had only been in her for a matter of minutes but she could already feel that tugging in the pit of her belly, dark splotches building behind her vision as she peaked.

"I love you," he whispered reverently into the side of her lips, his voice so gentle it was in direct contrast to the way that he was handling her body, sending her spiraling even further. "But I'm not nearly done with you yet, beautiful girl." It was the kind of threat that she could appreciate, tumbling over that peak as he lifted her thigh just enough to send him even deeper inside of her, a long-drawn out moan working it's way out of her lips as he slammed into the back of her.

This, here, against this tree- this was fine. This could be her life. Full of blood and wolves and the things of her nightmares. The man who spun her roughly into her orgasm, the man who whispered love into her skin despite his harsh holds, that man could make it worth it.

Epilogue

It had been a month. A month of running through wooded areas and teaching Mabry how to live within the both of her skins now that they had gotten rid of the woman who had taken her in the first place. Horas hadn't expected the transition to suddenly just be easy because she had accepted him as her mate. If anything, he had expected that to make things harder.

And he had been right.

Mabry had fought changing again right up until she had been forced to do so, flashing from one skin to another and back again with just as brief of a space between as there had been the first time. Something that frustrated the both of them. She insisted that it wasn't something that they needed to work on, that if he loved her he would just accept it as it was now and not want anything else, but still he had pushed.

Just because Sasha was dead didn't mean that her pack had given up, he had no idea who her Beta had been or what his view on the matter would be- so they were still running. There was a pack further east that he knew would welcome them. An alpha he had personal experience with that he knew had experience in reluctant wolves.

For now though he was watching his mate dance about the edge of the river, her blonde hair shining in the afternoon sun as she splashed calf deep in the water. She was petulant, spoiled, and more than a little scatterbrained… but she was also incredibly intelligent, fiercely loyal, and extremely warm-hearted. She was nothing that he would have imagined his mate to be… But then, he hadn't ever really imagined one, and he was learning that she complemented him more than he would have thought imaginable.

"You're not going to swim with me?!" Mabry called, laughter in her tone as she splashed him ineffectively from where she stood, water barely even making it a few feet beyond her.

"Why? When I can watch you instead?" he called back, eyebrows raising at the way that she rolled her eyes.

"Maybe I'll just have to bring the water to you!"

"That's a feat that would be impressive," he snorted, unable to contain that grin that broke his lips at her threat.

Neither of them were able to hide that too obvious happiness in their expressions, or the joy that they were finding in one another.

Perhaps that was why they didn't see the figure several yards back, peering around a tree at them with violence riddling his gaze and malice stemming from his very core.

THE END

Printed in Great Britain
by Amazon